May we always remember
that each new day is something
to be excited about.

I Love Waking Up With You

by Nicole Sc tty Trumble

ISBN 978-1-7355818-0-4 paperback;
978-1-7355818-1-1 kindle eBook;
978-1-7355818-2-8 ePUB

My house is dark and peaceful.

My family's all asleep.

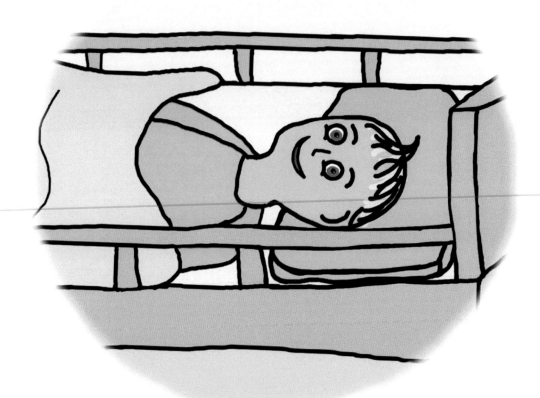

But my eyes just popped open.

So I <u>kick</u> away my sheets.

I glance up at my clock
to make sure it's morning time.

Then I bolt up to my knees
to shout out my favorite lines...

"Mommy!
It's morning time!"

"Time to wake up!"

I hear her slowly rustling
through her door and towards my bed.

"Good morning my sweet boy,"
is the kind of thing she says.

Though her stride is a bit sleepy,
I can see she's quite awake.

For her eyes twinkle with brightness
when she sees my smiling face.

She tickles me with kisses
as she lifts me to her chest.

She reminds me that I fill her up
with love and happiness.

To the stairs we stroll together,
nestled gently cheek to cheek.

Then years later, hand in hand,
while pets scamper through our feet.

On the couch we'll have a cuddle
before starting the day new.

And my mother always tells me
"I love waking up with you."

The End

Made in the USA
Columbia, SC
29 January 2021